The very ugly bug
F-J PIC

46829

This book belongs to

_____

_____

_____

To Ella
who is a beautiful
butterfly

tiger tales
an imprint of ME Media, LLC
202 Old Ridgefield Road, Wilton, CT 06897
This paperback edition published 2007
First published in the United States 2005
Originally published in Great Britain 2004
By Little Tiger Press
An imprint of Magi Publications
Text and illustrations copyright © 2004 Liz Pichon
ISBN-13: 978-1-58925-404-6
ISBN-10: 1-58925-404-X
Library of Congress Cataloging-in-Publication Data
Pichon, Liz.
   The very ugly bug / by Liz Pichon.
      p. cm.
   Summary: A bug is so ugly she scares away the bird that
was about to devour her.
   ISBN 10: 1-58925-048-6 (hardcover)
   ISBN 13: 978-1-58925-048-2 (hardcover)
   ISBN 10: 1-58925-404-X (paperback)
   ISBN 13: 978-1-58925-404-6 (paperback)
[1. Insects—Fiction. 2. Ugliness—Fiction.] I. Title.
PZ7.P5555Ve 2005

                                                   2004017277
         Printed in China
         1 3 5 7 9 10 8 6 4 2

The Very Ugly Bug

by Liz Pichon

tiger tales

There was once an ugly bug.
A **very** ugly bug.

All the other bugs were a bit ugly,
but she was by far the ugliest.

She had huge googly eyes,

a lumpy, wibbly-wobbly head,

a horrible hairy back,

and spotted purple legs.

What a sight she was!

Now you see me . . .

The very ugly bug wondered why the other bugs didn't look like her.

"Spotty red bug, why are your eyes so teeny tiny, and not big and googly like mine?"

"My eyes are teeny tiny so I can hide in the berries and be safe from birds," said the spotty red bug.

"Skinny green bug, why is your back so smooth and green, and not hairy like mine?" asked the very ugly bug.

"My smooth green back means I can hide in the leaves and be safe from birds," said the skinny green bug.

"Shiny blue bug, why do you have such big fluttery wings? I don't have any wings at all," said the very ugly bug.

"I use my big fluttery wings to fly away from birds, high up in the sky..."

Up, up, and away!

"like this!" said the shiny blue bug.

Whooooooooooooooooooosshhh!

fluttery wings, then I would be safe from birds, too.

So the very ugly bug decided that she would make a mask to help her eyes look teeny tiny.

She used a leaf
to make her back look
smooth and green.

She even found a
pair of fluttery
wings. "I'll be safe
from birds now!"
she said.

But she wasn't safe at all. The funny disguise made her stand out even more! Now everyone could see her—including a big, hungry bird in the sky.

Ta-da!

"Yum, yum," said the bird. "Look at that lovely juicy bug down there. It looks delicious!" And he flew down for a tasty bug snack.

"Argh!" yelled the very ugly bug as the bird swooped closer. The other bugs quickly hid and flew away. Then, suddenly, something very strange happened.

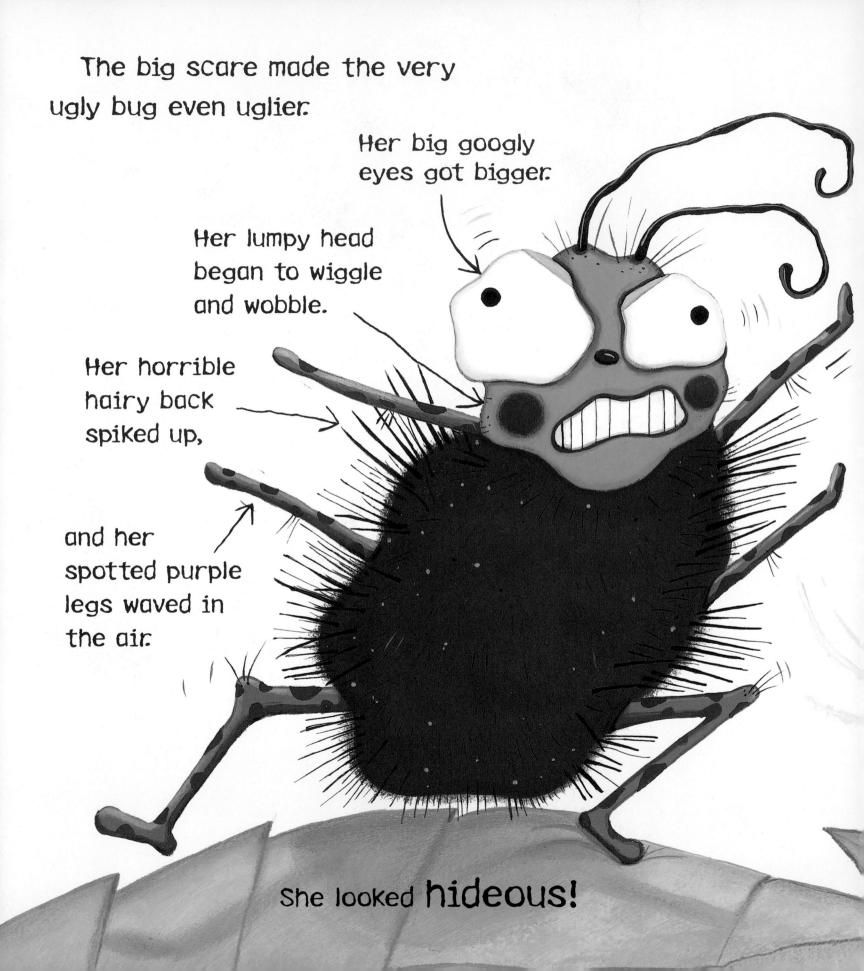

The big scare made the very ugly bug even uglier.

Her big googly eyes got bigger.

Her lumpy head began to wiggle and wobble.

Her horrible hairy back spiked up,

and her spotted purple legs waved in the air.

She looked hideous!

"Ugh," said the bird. "That bug doesn't look tasty at all! It will give me a tummy ache." And he flew off to look for a nice juicy caterpillar instead.

very ugly bug!"

cheered the other bugs. "She's so ugly she scared the bird away!"

"Now I love the way I look!" said the very ugly bug proudly. And Mr. Ugly Bug agreed. He thought she was gorgeous.

The two ugly bugs fell in love and had
a big family of baby bugs...

who were all even uglier than their parents!